BOUNDER'S ADVENTURES
IN HOMEHILL

Tales from Homehill | *Book One*

Bounder's Adventures in Homehill

written by Penny Shackleton

illustrated by Louise Byng

CONTENTS

Chapter 1 | Bounder Arrives in Homehill

Once upon a time there was a bunny called Bounder. He was a small brown rabbit with a white fluffy tail.

He lived in a little wooden house in Hutchanrun. Bounder's bedroom was upstairs. Once a week the boys who looked after him lifted out the old hay and put in new. This kept it smelling good and fresh. Each Saturday Bounder had the job of rearranging it. He made it into a nice comfy mattress and a nice comfy pillow. He had done it so often now; it only took him a few minutes to have it ready for the night.

Bounder ate downstairs. Oats, pellets and fresh new carrots appeared in his dish every morning and evening. His water bowl got refilled and the boys who looked after him shouted, 'There's some nice fresh water, Bounder.'

Outside his front door Bounder had a large enclosed pen. In the winter he just went for a quick run around, but in the summertime when it was warm and sunny he stayed outside for longer, basking in the sunshine and nibbling at the tender grass.

Occasionally the grass had the flavour of wild daisies and dandelions. But he never tasted their juicy flowers because his owners came out with a lawn-mower and cut them down long before they bloomed.

You would think that Bounder was a very happy and contented bunny. He had a lovely home and good food. Bounder knew he was well looked after. But he had a problem. Well two really.

The first was this. Every spring some good-looking flowers appeared just outside his run. They were bright yellow and had heads that danced in the wind. They looked very tasty. He longed to eat them.

When no one was around, he tried to reach them. He went to the far end of his run. Then he bounded towards them and leapt into the air. He was sure he could get to them if he really tried. And try and try and try he did, but it was always the same. He leapt up, hit his head on the wire netting and fell back down to Earth with such a bump.

He could not escape from his cage. Each spring he failed to reach and taste those lovely looking flowers.

The second problem was his dreams. They were really wild dreams. He dreamt he was bounding over hills, hills that went on for miles and miles and miles. Within those hills were streams of running water. Now when I say it was running, that's what I mean - it was running! It was alive! It was bubbly! It was fresh! It was cool and it tasted absolutely heavenly! What a drink!

Nothing like the water in his bowl in Hutchanrun – that was dull and boring. The grass and the flowers in his dreams were wild tasting too. They were so fresh and so new. They were great!

Oh, he felt so free, so alive. He could be himself. He could run and jump and leap for as long as he wanted. There were no fences, no netting, no boundaries to stop him - just miles and miles of open space. How he enjoyed himself.

But then, it was always the same. He woke up and found himself back in his straw bed. He had great fun running over those hills but he felt so sad when he woke and found out it was only a dream. Poor Bounder.

One spring day everything changed. He saw the flowers, he charged at them and leapt; and as he leapt, he felt as though he was flying.

Guess what?

He was flying.

When he landed he was not in his cage. He was beside those beautiful tasty yellow flowers. Was it a dream? He shook himself. Nothing changed. He shook himself again; still nothing changed. He shook himself again and again. Each time he expected to wake up in his bed of hay but he didn't. He was out in the open, next to the flowers. He shook himself just once more. Yippee! He was awake! He had escaped!

He turned and looked around. The wire netting that normally held him back had come loose and he could see the hole through which he had flown.

It was true! He was free! He had a quick nibble at the flowers. Oh how sweet and tasty they were! His next mouthful gave him a sense of adventure and freedom. He felt like he had super-springs on his hind legs. He was ready to fly.

Bounder bounced over the surrounding garden and squeezed through the neighbouring hedge. There was green pleasant grass all around. He was in the open countryside.

He felt free. He was free! He went bounding off over the hill.

Bounding, leaping, bounding and leaping over and over again. Higher and higher up the hill. Further and further away from Hutchanrun.

After a while he began to feel tired. He wandered over to a nearby tree and sat down in its shade. He was tired. He'd never had so much exercise before. He needed a rest so he sat there admiring the view.

The hills and grass went on forever. In the distance were purple mountains. Over to his left was a forest of green trees but to the right there were only a few trees here and there. Bright yellow bushes and the odd pile of stones dotted the landscape. A silver stream of running, shiny water cascaded down the hillside.

It was beautiful!

As he was sitting there, he heard a couple of voices behind him. He strained to listen to what they were saying and this is what he heard:

'No, I don't think we've seen him before.'

'He's not from our warren, but he looks a bit like us. Perhaps he's a distant cousin?'

'Are you sure he's wild? He looks rather tame to me.'

'Yes, look at the way his eyes sparkle. Tame rabbits don't look like that – although he does look rather well-groomed.'

'Well, dear, are you going to speak to him or shall I?' said the female voice. Bounder was about to turn round to see who was speaking, when suddenly he heard a thud. Thud, thud, thud.

There in front of him was a lovely doe looking straight into his eyes. She had a welcoming smile on her face and just as she was about to say hello, there was another thud and her buck appeared by her side. They looked a bit like Bounder although their eyes were more sparkly and their fur was longer than his and just a slightly different shade of brown. But they each had a fluffy white tail just like Bounder's.

'Hello, young chap,' said the doe. 'We were wondering if we'd seen you before. I'm Higher and this is my buck, Digger.'

'No, you'll not have seen me before. My name's Bounder and I've just arrived. I was living in Hutchanrun but I've bounded up the hill and here I am.'

'Well, good to see you, Bounder,' said Digger. 'Good name by the way. Do you have any warren to stay in or would you like to share ours?'

'Oooh, that would be good,' said Bounder. 'I kept dreaming I would escape from Hutchanrun. And here I am. I am free but homeless. I would love a place in your warren – that is, if you don't mind.'

'Of course we don't,' said Higher. 'We're always glad when other rabbits come to Homehill. Come and join us.'

'Thank you so much,' said Bounder and he followed them up the hill to their home.

So Bounder left Hutchanrun behind and joined the warren of Homehill. He began to live as a Homehill rabbit.

He found out through chatting to other rabbits that his great-grandparents had been part of Homehill Warren. His grandma had lived there too until one day she was caught in a poacher's trap.

Some humans found her and took her home. They cared for her until her leg was better. Then she was married to one of their Hutchanrun rabbits, Bounder's grandfather.

His mother was born to them. She married another Hutchanrun rabbit, Bounder's father. There was no freedom in Hutchanrun. The rules were strict and punishments severe.

Bounder's dad refused to let her talk about the Homehill side of her family. He thought that if she did not speak about Homehill things, she would forget about them. When she began to have bunkins (baby rabbits) he thought she must be truly settled in Hutchanrun.

But Bounder's mum never forgot her roots. She remembered and loved all the Homehill lullabies her mother had sung to her as a baby. As soon as her buck left their house and was out of earshot, she sang them all to baby Bounder; when he was around she spoke only of Hutchanrun things.

When Bounder was old enough to babble his mum had to stop singing. She knew if Bounder began to repeat Homehill songs they would both be beaten

to death and made into rabbit pie!

However she also knew the songs were special and that once Bounder had heard them they would stay in his heart and be part of him forever. This is why Bounder had his wild dreams. This is why he was now in Homehill.

As Bounder wandered around he found out lots of other things. He was told that Higher was so named because she could jump higher than any other rabbit in Homehill and had a gift of teaching others to do the same.

Digger was good at burrowing deeper and deeper into the ground. He found many gems and precious stones and was always ready to share them with others. The does made them into necklaces and the bucks made them into tie-pins. The gems were very precious to everyone in Homehill.

Bounder grew to love Homehill. Higher and Digger cared for him so very well and he became part of their family.

The flowers and grass in Homehill tasted wonderful. They were like those in his dreams. The streams that flowed down the hillside were amazing. They tasted so fresh and so free!

As he explored more he found that each stream had a different flavour and satisfied in a different way. As time went by he began to recognise each flavour. He knew where to go to quench the particular thirst he was feeling.

However, because he had not been born in Homehill he got himself into a few scrapes. But these are stories for another day.

Chapter 2 | Polka Dot Passion

Bounder woke up from a very good sleep and rubbed his eyes with his paws. He was feeling full of energy and bounce and ready for another adventure.

'Today is Saturday!' he thought. 'I wonder what the weather's like.'

He jumped out of bed and looked out the window. It was a beautiful day. The sun was shining. The sky was blue and cloud-free.

'What a great day to explore,' he said to himself.

He had a quick drink of carrot juice and left the warren. He decided to visit a new part of Homehill. So he bounded up the hill outside the warren until he came across a path he had not seen before. He followed it.

After a little while the path ran alongside a gentle stream.

He had not seen the stream either. He had not tasted or drunk its water. He wandered over and took a little sip. Ooh, it was so good. The water tasted like liquid gold. It was refreshing and cooling and sweet. He took another drink and licked his lips.

It was indeed very special water. It not only satisfied your thirst as you drank but it also created a thirst for more. 'Yummy, yummy, yummy!' he said to himself, 'I must get to the top, I must find the source.' For every rabbit knows, the closer you get to the source of a stream, the purer the water is. If the water here, half way down the hill, is this good then at its source, at the top of the hill, it must be absolutely heavenly.

So Bounder bounded and leapt and ran up the hill, following the path of the stream. After a while he slowed down. He needed a rest. The sun was high in the sky and he was hot. Although he had had plenty to drink, he was now beginning to feel hungry.

He looked around for a comfy place to stop. A little distance away from the path was a tree. He decided to go over and rest in its shade.

'What a lucky bunny I am,' he said to himself. 'Just look at these - yummy, yummy, yummy. Dinner, here I come!'

For underneath the tree were some very tasty looking mushrooms. These were not like the plain brown ones growing in the foothills. They were bright red and speckled with little white spots.

They looked so good. He began to nibble away at the largest one. He was right, it was yummy. He nibbled away until his tummy was full. Then he decided it was time for an after-dinner nap. He curled up in the shade of the tree and fell fast asleep.

Oh dear! After a short while he woke with a start. Ooh! Ouch! He didn't know what was happening. His tummy felt like someone was stabbing him with a red-hot poker. His mouth felt like sandpaper and he was desperate for a drink.

When he tried to stand, his legs were like jelly. He could not move. What was he going to do? Why did he feel so bad?

He could hear the stream bubbling in the distance. It was only about a hundred hops away but he could not even manage a little jump.

As he was wondering what to do he fell asleep again. That made things worse! He began to dream. He was being chased by big white rabbits. They were throwing cabbages at him. One of them was chasing him with a lasso and another one was carrying a wire-netting cage.

'We've come to collect you! You didn't think your trip to Homehill was forever did you?' the first one yelled.

'Back to Hutchanrun for you!' said the other.

Just as he saw the noose coming over his head, he woke up with a start.

'Oh, it was just a dream!' he said, rubbing his eyes with his front paws. He nearly fell over. His back paws were too wobbly to support him.

He looked at the mushroom he had nibbled.

'Was it something to do with this?' he wondered. But then he told himself, 'Something so tasty could not be so bad.' He was just about to take another mouthful when he fell back to sleep.

The white rabbits returned. This time they caught him. He couldn't move. They lifted him up and then he felt himself falling. They had put him in the cage. He watched. The lid was almost shut.

Then he woke up! He sighed. 'Oh, it was only a dream!'

He smiled again. His tummy began to rumble. He was hungry. He was just about to take another bite of the yummy mushroom when he heard a shout.

'Stop! Bounder! Don't!' Up bounded Higher and knocked him over.

She took one look at him. 'Oh, I can see I'm too late,' she said. 'How much did you eat - and why?'

'I only took a little nibble,' he said. She stared at him suspiciously.

'Well, it was lunch-time and it looked so tasty.

I had a few mouthfuls . . . a good few mouthfuls. Well, all right. Actually, I ate a lot, but it doesn't matter. It's a very good tasting mushroom - better than the ones at the bottom of the valley,' Bounder said nervously.

'And do you feel good now?' Higher replied. Bounder shook his head. She continued, 'Do you think perhaps the mushroom has something to do with how you're feeling? Something to do with the dreams?'

'No. How can it?' said Bounder, 'I'm just hot and tired. I've come a long way, you know. It's nothing to do with the mushroom. See how good it looks.'

'Well, if you want to believe that, do so. But I know what those mushrooms can do,' said Higher.

'I don't believe you,' said Bounder. 'I was hungry and mushrooms are good to eat. See how lovely that one looks. Yummy, yummy. It can't cause nasty dreams. It has to be the heat and the sun.'

'Well, if you still want to believe that, it's up to you. But I am telling you it is the mushroom.'

Bounder was looking at the mushroom and shaking his head.

'It was yummy, not nasty. How can you say that?'

'I do know and I will help you if you would like me to. But if you don't, then I'll leave you alone, with your dreams and your delicious mushroom.'

Bounder was feeling sorry for himself. He had been pleased when Higher arrived but he did not agree with what she was saying. Neither did he want her to leave. He didn't want to be alone again.

'Oh, please don't go, Higher. It's just that I was hungry. It was lunchtime and the mushroom looked so tasty. I didn't know it would make me feel like this. No one told me. Would another little nibble really hurt?'

He looked at Higher. She looked at him. Their eyes met. He didn't know what to do. It was as though he was a baby bunny again and his mother was singing the melodies which stirred his heart to dream of distant lands. Those feelings which had been awakened in his heart when he was in Hutchanrun came flooding back. He knew Higher cared for him and was telling the truth.

'Oh Higher, what have I done! I so want to live and be a Homehill Rabbit, but perhaps I'll never learn. Perhaps I should just go back to my old house and be content with dead water and good carrots and oats. Life was simple there and my tummy never hurt like this.'

'I've told you, I can make the pain stop if you would like me to,' said Higher. 'But you have to make that choice. Come with me further up the hill.'

And off she went.

Bounder watched as she set off up the hill. The path looked very steep. He was left all by himself, lonely, sore and very tired. But he decided to follow.

He crawled after Higher. His back legs were wobbly and his tummy ached but he followed her up the hill.

Up and up they went.

Higher was leaping and bounding but Bounder trailed slowly behind her.

Higher stopped when she realised Bounder was not keeping up with her. 'Come on, Bounder,' she said. 'Live up to your name. You can climb quicker than this.'

'But, Higher,' he said, 'I'm hungry. I'm tired. My tummy hurts and I don't know if I can or if I want to. . . .'

Higher looked at him again; her heart was sore. She could tell he was in trouble and she knew how he could be made better.

He had to climb to the source of the Polka Dot Stream and drink of its water. But it would only make him well if he made the journey himself.

She could not carry him. How could she encourage him? Bounder was losing heart. He looked as though he was ready to give up.

What could she do?

Then she remembered.

She could see by his eyes he was a Homehill rabbit. And Homehill rabbits find life in Homehill songs. So she began to sing:

'I have a place, a place on this hill,
Where the flowers grow, and my heart is still.
It's where I belong, it's where my heart dwells.
This is my place of rest.

Do you know Homehill? That place on the hill,
Where the flowers grow, and your heart is still.
It's a place of rest, a place called Home,
Where you can return each night.

Let your wanderings cease, find that place on
the hill,
Where the flowers grow, and your heart is still.
It's the place of rest, just made for you,
This place that is called Homehill.'

It worked. The song made Bounder weep. Little tears ran down his cheeks.

'Oh, Higher, what have I done? I thought living here would be so good, so much fun and so easy. But I've only been here a short while and I've managed to get myself in a tangle. Freedom is not as good as I thought it would be. A nice cage and good food is better. At least when I was in Hutchanrun there was no pain.'

Suddenly up bounded Digger.

'Well, good to see you, Bounder. I was just saying to Higher this morning I had not seen you about today. Hey, you don't look well. Are you all right?'

'I am thinking about going home to Hutchanrun,' said Bounder.

'You can't be serious. Going home to Hutchanrun? What do you mean? Hutchanrun isn't your home. You belong to Homehill. Your heart is here, so home is here. Where else would you call home?

Hutchanrun?

'It was never the right place for you. Remember the netting, was it good? No. That's why you longed for freedom. Remember those longings? Do you know what they were? That was your heart. It was saying - "I don't belong here. I am restricted here. There's another place for me. I want to be free." Well, now you are. Good, safe food isn't everything, you know. The food here is wild and tasty refreshing and. . . .'

'. . . And painful and sick,' put in Bounder. 'At least carrots and oats don't make your tummy sore, your head hurt, your legs weak and . . . .'

'So you are going to give up the freedom, the fun, the life you've found here, just because you've had a bite of a polka dot mushroom and can't be bothered to climb up the hill to the source of Polka Dot Stream? Look, we're almost there . . . and you don't know what awaits you when you drink . . . heaven's not the word for it. It's . . . well, find out for yourself. Here we are. If you stand on that rock there, you can bend forward and take a good long drink.'

Bounder looked around. He hadn't realised that as they'd been talking, they'd also been climbing. He was at the source of the stream. He looked down.

It was crazy. It was as though the water coming out of the ground and flowing down the hill was full of red and white polka dots.

It reminded him of the 'tasty' mushroom he'd nibbled at just about an hour ago. Well, if polka dot mushroom made him so ill, he certainly was not going to drink polka dot water.

'You've fooled me, haven't you?' he said sulkily.
'I thought you were friends. I trusted you and
you expect me to drink that!'

'It's the cure, for a polka dot tummy, polka dot legs and polka dot thoughts,' said Digger. 'Do you want to keep your sore tummy forever or are you going to drink?'

Bounder looked at Digger in disgust. He was just going to run back down the hill when . . . thud . . . splash!

He found himself in the middle of the flowing stream with a mouthful of dots. Higher had crept up behind him and given him a shove. She knew he had to choose to drink himself but knew he needed help.

Higher knew if Bounder was in the middle of the stream with a mouth full of dots, he would either have to swallow them or spit them out. She guessed that since Bounder was too polite to spit them out he would have to swallow them. She was right.

Bounder swallowed a mouthful of dots. He was surprised. The dots were delightful. They were like fizzy sherbert fountains, sweet carrotade and tender spring grass all rolled into one. After he swallowed the ones in his mouth he put his head in the water for another mouthful and another and another.

Then he began to laugh. He dived and swam in the water. He called out to Higher and Digger,

'Do come and join me. This is fun.' Digger and Higher jumped in beside him and they had a great time in the river.

After a while, Bounder realised he was no longer feeling poorly. His hunger had gone, his thirst was quenched and the power was back into his paws. He was able to splash and swim with the others. He had to agree with Higher and Digger - polka dot water is great!

After some time they decided to paddle downstream back to their warren. Digger, the grown up buck, paddled faster than Bounder and Higher. He arrived home first and disappeared into his room.

'Don't go away,' he shouted. 'I'll be back in a minute.' After a lot of scurrying and rustling, he came out with a parcel. 'For you, my chap,' he said, handing Bounder a box.

Bounder took the box and opened it. There inside was a beautiful tie-pin with a gem of a stone which sparkled in the sun.

It was bright red and covered in little white polka dots.

'It's been made just for you,' said Higher, pinning it on his tie. 'To remind you of today. You have received a very important treasure and learnt a very important lesson. You know how to drink from Polka Dot Stream. That stream will fill your heart when you are hungry and full of longing.'

'But that's not true' said Bounder. 'I didn't learn anything. I ate of the. . . . '

'No, it's very true' said Digger. 'You felt a hunger, you ate and were filled. The fact that you took a slight detour does not really matter. Keep this pin close to your heart. It will remind you of today. Whenever you feel that same hunger and longing in your heart go to Polka Dot Stream at the top of the hill. Jump in, drink and enjoy. It will never fail. It will always satisfy.

'Don't go for the mushrooms! They are second-best. Go for the real stuff.

It's a bit more of a climb, but worth the effort, don't you think?'

Bounder had to agree. That night as he snuggled down to sleep, he gazed at the jewel in his tie-pin and sang the Homehill song.

Chapter 3 | Forlorn Hill

Bounder often went back to Polka Dot Hill and enjoyed drinking from Polka Dot Stream. From there he also explored other hills. He liked visiting Purple Heather Hill and Sweet Grass Hill.

As he looked into the distance from them he could see the summit of yet another hill. It was not quite as bright and sunny as the others. In fact the hill looked a bit forlorn. But that was not going to put him off. He had decided that one day he would also climb to the top of it.

It was now the middle of summer. The days were warm and sunny and the evenings were cool and balmy. Daylight hours stretched out into late evening so there was plenty of time to explore.

Bounder decided this was a good time to go to the summit of that distant hill. He set off from his warren and ran over to Sweet Grass Hill. From there he bounded on and on. At times he stopped to admire the view, to drink from the pleasant running streams and to nibble at the tasty grass.

He began to sing as he went:

"I'm a Homehill bunny on the run,
I'm exploring the hills, oh what fun!
With a run, with a jump,
With a leap and with a bound,
I am amazed at the things I have found.

Water that's alive flowing down and down,
Sweetest-tasting grass growing all around,
Flowers fair, trees so tall,
Help arriving when you call,
Life has joy, it's a thrill,
In this place that's called Homehill
Where our hearts find their rest and are still."

As he climbed higher towards Forlorn Hill he noticed it looked like its name - forlorn. He wondered if he should go on. But he knew he was born for adventure and that included visiting new places. He climbed and jumped and grazed and drank. A bit further on, he came across a well-travelled path. It was made of purple-blue shale and was hard on his paws. 'At least it shows me the way to go,' he thought. 'It has to lead to somewhere.'

So he bounded along it. He found the grass at the side of the path was not quite as tasty as that on Homehill. It was more difficult to chew. His jaws must be getting as tired as well as his paws!

He drank from the stream that ran alongside the path. The water was not fresh. There was no life in it but he was thirsty so he continued to drink. It tasted quite stale and reminded him of something he'd drunk before.

'Ah yes,' he thought, 'it's like Hutchanrun water.'

He began to sing. . . .

'Hutchanrun water and Hutchanrun food,
Hutchanrun home and Hutchanrun bed.'

Slower and slower he moved. He was dreaming of the 'good old days'. He remembered how water just appeared on his table, and how oats, pellets and carrots were placed in his dish each day without having to hunt for them.

The sun was setting. He gave a little shiver. It was getting chilly and now it was time for bed. He realised that he was surrounded by shale. There was no place to dig a little burrow for a bed. He moved the shale to one side in the hope of finding earth but he just came up against hard, solid rock.

Then, plop, plop, plop. The rain started. Plop, plop, plop. He looked around for somewhere to shelter but there was nowhere.

The place was desolate. No trees, no shrubs, not even a little grassy area to provide a soft cushion for his head. The wind began to blow, the mist drifted in and the rain continued. Bounder soon became a very, wet, cold, forlorn bunny.

Oh how he dreamt of his nice warm, comfortable place in Hutchanrun. 'Why did I ever leave?' he thought. 'I had two-legged friends, all the food I could ever need and safety and comfort every day. I'm not a Homehill bunny after all. Homehill is home for Higher and Digger because they were born here. But it's not my home. I'm just a Halfling, well Quarterling really. Three of my grandparents were Hutchanrun rabbits; it was only my grandmother who was from Homehill. My home is in Hutchanrun and how I wish I was there just now.'

Little tears fell from his eyes and joined the rain that was already soaking his fur. He looked all around. The light was failing so he could no longer see the path that he'd been following. He was lost. He was alone. He was cold, hungry and friendless. He fell asleep dreaming of his nice warm bed in Hutchanrun.

When he woke his legs were stiff, his fur damp and his paws sore. When he opened his eyes he was surprised to discover he was not in his hutch. Where was he?

Then he remembered. He was lost. The rain had stopped, but there was still a lingering mist. He could not see where to go. There was no food and no drink and no shelter.

'So much for adventure,' he thought. 'I've had enough. I'll go back and tell Higher and Digger I'm going home. But why?' he said to himself. 'Why tell them? They'll only try and persuade me to stay in this cold forlorn place. They don't care about me anyway. They just want me to help them dig their warren and increase their store of winter food.

'No. Forget them. I can manage by myself. I can and I will look after myself. It's back to Hutchanrun for me. Homehill was a nice holiday place - a lovely place for the summer. Now that winter is approaching I will be better off living in Hutchanrun.'

He gazed through the mist and worked out the way he should go.

As he looked across to the other side of the hill he saw a stream he recognised from the 'good old days'.

'Go straight down the hill,' he told himself, 'and then, if you follow Stale Water Stream you should arrive at Hutchanrun in no time.'

So he set off. He bounded down the hill. Well, he was not really bounding, more sliding and slithering. There was not a proper path and if he landed on the smaller pieces of shale he started an avalanche and had to go where he was taken. After a while the shale pieces became more scattered. He felt bits of rough grass under his paws.

He then saw Stale Water Stream. All the streams in Homehill had nice wide paths at either side so he looked for the one at the edge of Stale Water. For some reason there wasn't a path either on Bounder's side of the stream or on the opposite bank. He did not understand that Homehill bunnies would not want to walk beside Stale Water Stream. And they certainly wouldn't want to drink from it.

Bounder decided they were either too lazy to make one or hadn't yet got round to it, since it was on the outskirts of Homehill.

Maybe the pathmakers had it on their list as their next project. The way was very overgrown and he had to crawl along through the undergrowth.

As he struggled he began to complain. 'Lazy Homehill rabbits. Fancy not putting a path here. How can they be so slow? They should have cut down these thistles by now. Lazy creatures!'

He muttered to himself all the time he was crawling along the side of the stream. Then he came across a patch of nettles. His fur protected him from some of the sting, but there were a few tender places, like his paws and the inside of his ears where the nettles touched and blistered.

But he was a brave, determined, stubborn rabbit. He knew this was the path back to Hutchanrun and that was where he was going. Nothing would stop him. Not even the thought that Homehill had nice soft grass to bound over.

At last he reached familiar territory. There was the outer field, the inner field and the hedge. 'I'm home at last,' he said to himself. 'Well, I'm back.' On the shale at the top of Forlorn Hill Hutchanrun had seemed the best place to be.

Now he had arrived, Hutchanrun did not seem that pleasant. But it was too late to change his mind, so he squeezed through the hedge and back into the garden.

When he saw the familiar row of yellow flowers nodding in the breeze he remembered how he used to dream and yearn for freedom. He knew he had tasted it in Homehill. He was feeling that same longing in his heart. He chose to ignore it!

'Back to my hutch I come,' he said. He looked and blinked and looked again. Maybe he'd taken a wrong turn and gone into the wrong garden. There was no hutch! He went back through the hedge and tried again.

The rows of yellow flowers were on his left and the hutch was straight ahead. But there was no hutch! So he tried again.

He went through the hedge a little further along and he found himself in the middle of a different lawn. After a few attempts at running backwards and forwards he realised the terrible truth. His hutch had been taken away. He could not go back. He was shocked. He crawled back through the hedge and sat down.

'What can I do? What am I going to do? Help me someone!' he cried.

Thump, thump.

Suddenly Digger and Higher were there.

'You called,' they said in unison.

'Oh, I didn't want you,' he said grumpily.

'Well, goodbye then,' they said and set off up the hill.

Bounder watched them. They were bounding up the hill. They had a spring in their step. They were free, free, free! He watched them again. He could feel the freedom they had. Watching them the longing stirred in his heart yet again.

He began to sing to himself:

'Life has joy, it's a thrill,
In this place that's called Homehill.
Water that's alive flowing down and down,
Sweetest-tasting grass growing all around. . .'

He continued singing till all the words of the song came back to him.

"I'm a Homehill bunny on the run,
I'm exploring the hills, oh what fun!
With a run, with a jump,
With a leap and with a bound,
I am amazed at the things I have found.

Water that's alive flowing down and down,
Sweetest-tasting grass growing all around,
Flowers fair, trees so tall,
Help arriving when you call,
Life has joy, it's a thrill,
In this place that's called Homehill
Where our hearts find their rest and are still."

And as he sang the last line, he realised that it was true. He heart had found its resting place. Homehill was where he belonged.

So he followed Higher and Digger up the hill.

'Wait for me!' he cried as he bounded after them. To this day he does not know how he managed to catch up with them but he did. 'I'm coming too!'

They stopped.

'Of course you are,' said Digger. 'This is your home. Where else would you go?'

'But I told you to go away.'

'Of course you did,' said Higher.

'Then why did you wait for me?' said Bounder. As he was speaking, he realised that he hadn't really caught them up. They had waited for him. He looked at Higher, she looked at him.

'Because you are Bounder,' she said.

As she spoke his name, he realised the truth. This was who he was. This was what he was made for. He was born for the hills. He was born for adventure. He was Bounder, the one who bounds!

Chapter 4 | Bounder Meets Hardy

It was a beautiful spring Monday morning. Bounder bounded over the hills towards the west of Homehill. He came across a group of young rabbits whom he hadn't seen before. They looked as if they were having fun, collecting flowers and chattering away to each other.

Bounder stood and watched. Every so often they disappeared over the brow of the hill with a bunch of flowers and then returned empty-pawed.
Bounder wondered what they were doing with the flowers. So he climbed to the top of the hill and looked over.

Half way down the other side of the hill was a large flat stone. On it lay a large pale grey-brown rabbit. He looked very important, very grown up and very well-educated. He was dressed in a smart brown jacket and had a top hat perched on his head. A flask of carrot juice sat by his side and he was sucking on a carrot-root lollipop.

The smaller rabbits were giving him the flowers they had picked. He inspected them, threw some away and placed the rest in a bucket at the side of the rock. It held a lot of daisies, some dandelions and a few buttercups.

Bounder had wandered down the hill so he was now quite close to the stone. Suddenly the large rabbit looked up, spotted him and spoke.

'Well, hello, young bunny. I don't think I've seen you in Mustimount before. You new around here?'

'Yes, I am. I'm Bounder. I've come to stay in Homehill.'

'Welcome, Bounder, nice to meet you. I'm Hardy and the lillle bunkins dashing around here are my class. Would you like to join us? You could be a real help to me and I would love to have you.'

'What would I need to do, Mr Hardy?' said Bounder.

'Oh, no need to call me Mr,' laughed Hardy. 'I'm just Hardy. We are gathering flowers for tomorrow's market. The bunkins are a great help to me so I give them twenty pence for every bunch they pick. I make sure the flowers are perfect and I sell them for three pounds a bunch.'

Bounder had not had any money before and twenty pence sounded a huge amount to him.

He said eagerly, 'Yes, Hardy, I would love to join your class. When can I start and what do I need to do?'

'Well,' said Hardy, 'you can join us right now. All you need to do is pick as many flowers as you can. You can start with the easy ones. Do you know what daisies look like?'

Bounder nodded.

'Brilliant!' said Hardy rubbing his paws together. 'Well, they're tiny flowers so we sell them in bunches of twenty. Rabbits only buy really good ones so you need to make sure the ones you pick don't have missing or broken petals.'

'OK,' said Bounder, thinking this was going to be an easy way to earn some money.

'I'll be here till four o'clock this afternoon. Gather as many flowers as you can and then bring them to me a bunch at a time.'

'OK, Hardy.'

'Well then, don't waste time talking. Off you go.' Hardy dismissed Bounder with a wave of his paw.

Bounder joined the others as they scurried around gathering flowers.

He ran up and down the hill picking daisies as he went. He inspected them carefully as he gathered them and collected the best ones he could find.

He made sure there were no missing, broken or discoloured petals. Before long he had gathered his first twenty.

'Well,' he said to himself, 'that was a quick way to earn twenty pence. I'm sure I'll make a pound before the day is over.'

He looked around. He was quite a way from the flat topped rock and there were lots of daisies between him and Hardy. He decided he would pick another bunch on the way back to the stone. He held one in each paw and took them to Hardy.

Hardy accepted the first one then threw the second one down on the ground. He then jumped and trampled on it. Bounder stared at him with his mouth open.

'Why have you done that?' he screamed.

'Bounder dear, a bunch at a time is what I said and a bunch at a time is what we collect.'

'But what's wrong with collecting two at once? It would save so much time.'

'I said a bunch at a time, and that's what I meant. That is how we do it, isn't it Petal?' Hardy said, turning to the young doe that had just appeared with a fine bunch of dandelions in her paw.

'Yes, Hardy, that is how we do it,' said Petal. She looked down her nose at Bounder, 'One bunch at a time.'

'Thank you, Petal dear,' Hardy said. He turned and put her bunch carefully in the bucket of water sitting in the shade under the stone. Petal hurried away.

Hardy then began to very carefully inspect the daisies which Bounder had brought.

'Well, I suppose they'll do for a first attempt,' he said, as he dismissed Bounder with a wave of his paw.

'What about my twenty pence?' said Bounder.

'Oh, not now, dear. We don't stop work till four o'clock. Then I'll add it all up and pay you at the end.'

Bounder did not look too pleased and was just going to go away when Hardy said, 'But since it's your first bunch, I'm sure I could bend the rules. Here you are, Bounder.' Hardy handed Bounder the shiniest twenty pence piece he had ever seen.

'Oh, thank you, Hardy,' he said. 'I'm off to get my next bunch,' and off Bounder bounded, singing to himself, 'One bunch at a time, for a twenty pence piece.'

He soon managed to collect another twenty daisies and this time he remembered the rules and took them to Hardy.

'Here you are, bunch number two.'

Hardy took the flowers from Bounder. He inspected them again.

'That one's no good. Look, there's a bent petal' he said as he threw it on the ground.

After a few minutes Hardy gave Bounder his bunch of flowers back. Bounder looked, took them away and counted them. He had seven left from the bunch he had given to Hardy. The rest had been thrown on the ground.

Well Bounder was a stubborn rabbit and he was determined to earn a pound before the day was out. So off he scampered, looking for the best daisies he could find. Backwards and forwards he went. By lunch time he had managed to collect another twenty pence worth and he was beginning to feel very tired. He went over to Hardy and asked for his money.

'Money?' roared Hardy. 'It's only one o'clock and you want your money? You have another three hours work . . . er . . . fun time left. Bounder, you can't stop now. Another three bunches and you will earn a shiny pound coin. Just think, a brand new, shiny pound coin for your pocket. I bet none of your friends have anything like that, do they?'

Bounder had to agree. None of his friends at Homehill ever had any money.

He was going to be the best. Just think how proud he would be when he went home with his shiny pound coin.

'Well, do you think I could have a drink? I'm hot and tired and I see you have flasks of carrotade beside you, Mr Hardy, sir.'

Hardy shook his head.

'Oh, Bounder. I couldn't give you any of that. You see, I'm an old rabbit and I need to keep drinking, otherwise I'll get a sore head. I get very hot sitting in the sun, waiting for you and all the others to bring me flowers. You wouldn't like me to be ill, now, would you?'

Bounder was a kind rabbit so he didn't want anyone to be ill. But he was also very thirsty.

'I only want a sip, sir, please?'

'A sip! Just a sip! What would happen if I gave you a sip? Everyone else would want one too. My carrotade would disappear in no time. No use at all, no use at all.'

Just then another rabbit appeared with a bunch of dandelions.

'Peter, dear. Do you think you could possibly take Bounder to the nearest stream? He's feeling a bit thirsty.'

'Of course, Hardy,' said Peter. 'I'll do anything you ask. You know that, don't you?'

'Of course, Peter. You're my best young rabbit. Here's fifty pence for your flowers.'

Hardy handed Peter a shiny fifty pence coin, which he took and put in his pocket. Bounder was just about to open his mouth to say something when Peter took hold of his paw and pulled him down the hill.

They jumped and bounded along and soon came to little stream. The water looked inviting so they bent down and had a drink. Bounder was not sure he liked the taste of it. It was a bit stale and lifeless, but he was very thirsty so he took another few big mouthfuls.

Soon he got used to the taste and it did quench his thirst.

'How did you manage to get your money?' said Bounder to Peter. 'I was told I had to wait until the end of the day.'

'Oh,' said Peter. 'I'm Hardy's star pupil today. Each week he chooses someone to be his star. We get paid fifty pence for each bunch as we collect them. It's great fun. Perhaps if you stay around long enough, you'll be Hardy's star. You are going to come back next week, aren't you? We'd love to have you helping us again.'

Bounder had planned to leave once he got his money, but Peter treated him so kindly and began to tell him wonderful stories of his adventures with Hardy and the class that he began to change his mind.

'Well, perhaps I will. I do enjoy collecting flowers,' said Bounder, 'perhaps I'll try dandelions next week.' They finished drinking.

'Do you know your way back?' said Peter. Bounder nodded. 'See you later then,' and away Peter went.

The daisies were more plentiful on this part of the hill. Bounder collected as many as he could and soon his paws were full. He knew he had to take them to

Hardy a bunch at a time, so he looked around. To his left there was a little bush. He laid all his daisies under it and then formed a bunch of twenty. He ran over to Hardy and handed it over. Hardy said it was perfect so Bounder ran back to his secret store.

Just before he reached it, he was stopped. Billy and Berty, another two of Hardy's class stood in his way. 'Sorry, you can't come this way,' said Berty.

'But I've come to get more of my daisies,' said Bounder. 'I left a pile here so I could give them to Hardy a bunch at a time.'

'Your daisies?'

'I left them here and I've come to collect them. I only need one more bunch to get my pound. Please let me pass,' Bounder moved forward.

This time Billy put out a paw and stopped him.

'You can't mean those!' he said, pointing to the pile of daisies Bounder had left on the ground. 'These are ones we've just collected. You can't have those. Hardy does not like stolen daisies you know.'

'They are not stolen. Those are the ones I picked earlier, down by the stream. I left them here so I could take them over to Hardy one bunch at a time.'

'Berty, do you hear that? Bounder says he picked our daisies. What a liar!'
Berty agreed with Billy.

'Yes Bounder,' he said, 'you must be mistaken. Perhaps you've come down the wrong path.'

Bounder protested. 'I left them by this bush. I collected them this afternoon and I mean to take them to Hardy and get my money.' He pushed past them. As he bent down Billy and Berty grabbed him and pushed him to the ground.

Although it was two against one, Bounder put up a good fight. They kicked and wrestled and fought. Berty soon realised that Bounder was not going to give in easily.

He suddenly stopped fighting, reached into his pocket and took out a flask of carrot juice. 'Anyone for a drink?' Billy and Bounder disentangled themselves.

'Ooh, yes please,' they said together. As they passed the flask around Berty came up with a plan.

'Look here,' he said. 'We know the daisies are ours but Bounder says they are his. If we keep on fighting they will all get squashed and none of us will have any flowers that Hardy will accept. Why don't we share them? A bunch each? Bounder will then get his pound.'

Bounder began to think about his shiny pound coin. He knew it was not fair. He knew Berty was telling lies, but what could he do?

'OK,' said Bounder.

'If we must,' said Billy.

The bunnies shook paws, tidied themselves up and began to share out the flowers. Just then a whistle blew.

'Too late. Let's go.' Berty took them both by a paw and dragged them up the hill to Hardy. Other little bunnies came scampering from all directions. Bounder and the class gathered around Hardy.

Hardy called out their names and the amount of money they were due. He handed it to them. If it was less than a pound the poor rabbit got booed but if it was more than a pound the others gave him a cheer.

Bounder waited for his name to be called. He was hoping for a cheer.

'And our newcomer, Bounder, deserves a cheer,' said Hardy, in a tone of voice that needed to be obeyed. 'He's made a grand total of eighty pence.'

The rabbits cheered. But Bounder was upset. A tear escaped down his cheek when he went to collect his money.

'Oh dear Bounder, whatever is the matter?' said Hardy.

'N . . . n . . . nothing,' said Bounder reaching out for his money.

'Eighty pence is a very good amount for a beginner,' said Hardy. 'I'll tell you what, if you bring it next week and collect one good bunch, I'll change those coins for a nice golden pound coin. In fact, I'll save a brand new, shiny one just for you. So dry your eyes, good lad. Cheer up and we'll see you next week. Say goodbye to Bounder, folks.'

'Goodbye Bounder,' echoed his class.

'See you next week,' said Hardy.

'See you next week,' they echoed.

'For a brand new, shiny pound coin.'

'For a brand new, shiny pound coin,' they all echoed.

Bounder set off home. His paw held his eighty pence but his head held a shiny, new pound coin.

'Just wait till Higher and Digger see what I've earned,' he thought as he bounded back to Homehill. 'Next week I shall get a pound coin, perhaps if I try really hard I could get two.'

Higher was in the kitchen when Bounder arrived.

'Welcome home, Bounder,' she said. 'Tea's just about ready. Good to see you again. Have you had a good day?'

'I've had a great day,' said Bounder. 'I've been . . .' then he stopped. Suddenly he felt as though Higher may not approve of what he'd been doing. 'I've just been wandering around, in the sunshine, finding new places and things like that.'

'Did you meet anyone on your travels? There must have been a few rabbits out roaming on a day like today.'

'No, no one special,' said Bounder, hurrying into his room and hoping Higher didn't see the pawful of coins he was carrying.

Where could he put them? For some reason they didn't look quite as shiny as they did on Mustimount. He knew that if Higher saw them she would start asking questions he didn't want to answer.

He looked around his bedroom. The only place he could hide them was under his pillow. Four coins make your pillow a bit lumpy and Bounder didn't sleep too well for the following six nights.

Monday soon came round again. It was time to change his four twenty pence pieces for the new shiny pound coin he had been dreaming about all week.

When he woke, the sun was shining. He gathered up his money and set out for Mustimount. He soon came across Hardy and his class. They were so pleased to see him. He gave Hardy his eighty pence.

'Thanks, Bounder. Here's the shiny pound coin I have kept for you,' he said, slipping it out of his coat pocket. 'This will soon be yours.' He held the coin so it sparkled in the sunlight as he showed it to Bounder.

Bounder was encouraged to work really hard throughout the day. He ran back and forwards to Hardy and did not seem to notice how often his flowers were thrown to the ground. All poor Bounder thought about was that nice, shiny, sparkly pound coin.

When it got to the end of the day the class gathered round Hardy again.

'And Bounder has a grand total of two pounds and twenty pence.' The other rabbits cheered and Bounder took a bow. It made him feel so good and so clever.

'I have your name and two pounds twenty written in my book. If you keep going you could earn one of these,' said Hardy as he pulled a five pound note out from his pocket. It was a lovely shade of blue and had special pictures on it.

Hardy had no problem persuading Bounder to stay with them until he had earned the five pounds. He returned to Homehill empty pawed but this time his head was full of a sky-blue five pound note.

Hardy told Bounder that he and his class were planning to move on in a few weeks time, but he was sure Bounder could earn his five pounds before they left. When Bounder was on Mustimount he thought that Hardy was really nice. Once he was back in Homehill he thought differently. He was sure Higher would not approve of his new friend. Each week he found it harder to answer her motherly questions about his travels with an 'Oh, I've just been here and there.'

Sometimes if she caught his eye, Bounder thought that she could read his mind. Once or twice he was going to tell her the truth but he always kept quiet. He wrongly imagined she would put a stop to his Monday wanderings. Bounder decided to keep it a secret until he had his five pound note in his paw.

On the last Monday in May Bounder collected his last bunch of flowers. Hardy's class cheered and clapped as he received the five pound note. They said that if ever they were close to Homehill again they would come and visit.

'Please do. I'd love to see you all again,' shouted Bounder. He waved his paw and set off home. Every few bounds he stopped to have a good look at his crisp new five pound note. It was indeed a lovely shade of blue and there were pictures of hutches and houses on it.

He was busy admiring it as he walked down the path to the warren.

Freddy, one of Higher and Digger's bunkins, was with them in the garden. He saw Bounder's attention was taken up with the piece of paper he was carrying. Freddy decided to have some fun. He ran up to Bounder.

'This looks interesting, what is it?' he said snatching the five pound note out of his paw. 'Ugh! Where did you get that?' He handed it back to Bounder as though it was a piece of rubbish.

'It's a five pound note,' said Bounder. 'Isn't it nice and crisp and new? Hardy gave it to me. Don't you like it?'

'Like it? Of course I don't like it. It's horrible, it's disgusting, it's. . . .'

'It's nice and crisp and new and has lovely pictures of houses and hutches.'

'It's awful, it's disgusting! How could you bring that here?' Freddy screeched. At that point Higher came over to see what was going on.

'Boys, boys,' she said, taking one in each paw. 'What is all the fuss?'

'That,' said Freddy, pointing to the five pound note which was now lying on the ground.

Higher bent down to pick it up, just as a gust of wind caught it and carried it away. Bounder tried to run after it but his paw was firmly held by Higher.

'Let me go,' he screamed, kicking and shouting and fighting. The more he fought the firmer Higher held him. He watched his hard-earned money floating up the hill and out of sight. He burst into tears.

'Freddy, you are horrible. I never want to talk to you again. You've made me lose my hard-earned money. You don't know how hot and tired I got trying to find flowers that Hardy liked. It was awful. You'd collect twenty nice, perfect flowers and he would say half of them were no good. What a job I had trying to please him and earn my money. And now it's blown away in the wind!'

As Bounder listened to himself, he realised that he hadn't really enjoyed his days with Hardy's class. He burst into tears again.

This time Higher let go of his paw. She motioned to Digger and Freddy to go inside and start the tea.

'What was the problem, Bounder dear?' she said putting a firm paw around Bounder's shoulders.

'I . . . I . . . I've lost my nice crisp five pound note. Freddy pinched it from me and then said it was rubbish and now it's blown away in the wind and I shall never get it back.'

'A nice crisp five pound note! What's a five pound note?'

'It's what you earn by helping Hardy. He was the beautiful rabbit I met in Mustimount. I collected flowers for him and that was my reward and now that bunkin of yours has made me lose it. It's not fair! You'll have to make him give me one of his. It was his fault it got blown away in the wind. You will make him do that, won't you, Higher?'

Bounder wiped away his tears, looked into Higher's eyes and smiled as nicely as he could.

'A five pound note? What makes you think Freddy has a five pound note? What makes you think anyone at Homehill has a five pound note? Why do you want one?'

'It was nice and crisp and blue. And I earned it, Higher. I worked ever so hard. Ever so hard! Hardy was so hard to please. You had to make sure that every flower you picked was perfect; he didn't like broken or crushed ones. That was my reward. I brought it home to show you. I was so proud. I was going to buy something nice with it.'

'Buy, five pound notes, what are we talking about?' Digger had come into the garden to tell them tea was ready. 'Bounder, have you seen any money in Homehill? Have you seen any shops? Have you seen anyone buying or selling things?'

'But it was nice and new and Hardy had saved it 'specially for me. I worked so hard; that was my reward,' said Bounder.

'But not necessary, Bounder,' said Digger. 'Money is not needed here. Money is not used in Homehill. We never want it to be. Everything on Homehill belongs to those who choose to live here. We share everything. Everything I have belongs to all who live here and everything Homehill rabbits have belong to us; the flowers, the grass, the hills, the streams, everything! It's all ours. Did you really enjoy your Mondays with Hardy? Was the water in the streams of Mustimount as good as our Polka Dot Stream? Were Billy and Berty better friends than our Freddy?'

Bounder looked at Digger.

'It's your choice, Bounder. Where do you belong? Mustimount, Hutchanrun or Homehill?'

He heard his mother's voice again, *'I have a place, a place on the hill…'*

He put one paw in Digger's paw and the other in Higher's and laughed.

'It was only a silly bit of blue paper, I'm glad it got blown away. Do you think Freddy will still be my friend?'

'Of course I will,' shouted Freddy, who had just come into the garden. 'Tea's ready and waiting and I'm starving. Are you coming?'

Chapter 5 | Happy Homaday

Bang, bang, bang. 'Bounder! Bounder!' Bounder rubbed his eyes and listened. Bang, bang, bang. 'Bounder! Bounder!' It was only six o'clock in the morning. Someone was knocking on his bedroom door and calling his name.

'Okay! I'm coming!' he shouted as he climbed slowly out of bed. He opened the door and Freddy bounded in.

'Aren't you up yet? I thought you'd be washed, groomed and eager to go. I can't wait, can you? Aren't you excited?'

Bounder looked at the young buck. He had no idea why Freddy was so excited. 'Freddy, calm down,' he said, putting his paws on Freddy's shoulders. 'Now stop jumping up and down and please tell me what you're talking about. You wake me up in the middle of the night and go chattering on about a special day. Why should I be excited? What's going on? And why should I be up? It's only six o'clock!'

'I wanted to wake you at sunrise,

but dad and mum said I had to wait at least until six. I could hardly wait for the big hand on the clock to reach the twelve.' Freddy looked at Bounder, who was staring at him, mouth open and a frown on his forehead. 'You don't know do you? Oh, it's so exciting. I did not realise you didn't know. Oh, you're in for a treat. See you later!' and he was just about to fly out again when Bounder ran over to the door and banged it shut.

'Freddy, you can't do this. What are you talking about? You woke me up, gibbered away about a special day and are now going away without explaining what is going on. No you can't, I won't let you. You need to tell me what you are talking about.'

'Oops,' said Freddy, 'maybe it was meant to be a surprise - but no, my mum and my dad said I could wake you at six so it must be all right to tell you. I thought you knew, thought you would remember.'

'Remember what? Know what?' said Bounder. 'Please stop talking in riddles and explain what I should know!'

'Ooh, happy day, exciting day!' said Freddy and began to jump up and down again. Bounder looked at him. He would have to do something to calm Freddy down and to get him to explain what was going on. Bounder was getting hungry and thought that maybe if Freddy sat at the table with him, he would calm down enough to talk some sense.

'Have you had breakfast, Freddy? How about some carrot juice and sweet-grass flakes?'

'I had some with mum and dad before they went out, but I'm sure I can manage another bowl,' said Freddy. 'Sweet-grass flakes are my favourite.'

'Well, come and help,' said Bounder. So they went into the kitchen and prepared breakfast, Freddy doing little hops and skips as he went from the cupboard to the table and back again and muttering under his breath, 'So exciting, so exciting, I can't wait.'

When he had first woken, Bounder was annoyed with Freddy. He had only just come out of a nice dreamy sleep and Freddy had been chattering in his ears like an inter-city train ever since. But he liked Freddy a lot and couldn't stay angry with him for long. They sat down. After his first few sips of carrot juice, Bounder felt more awake. He was now ready to hear more.

'Well, I'm all ears,' he said.

'Oh, these are delicious,' said Freddy, tucking into his sweet-grass flakes. 'Wait till I've finished them, then I'll explain.' And from the way he gazed into the dish, Bounder knew he was not going to hear another word from Freddy until his bowl was empty.

'What a cheek.' he thought. 'He wakes me up in the middle of the night, jumps up and down, chatters away and now I'm ready to listen, he's shut up. Silly little bunkins!'

As he sat watching Freddy, Bounder suddenly realised that he wasn't really annoyed with the young buck. In fact, when he stopped to think about it, Freddy's excitement was catching. Now he was eager to know what it was all about.

He was sure it was something good. It was about him and it was going to be exciting.

What day was it? Spring, number 20. Number 20, Spring. 20? 20? Yes, it did seem as though there was something special about this day. What was it? And as he chewed on his sweet-grass flakes he began to chew things over in his mind. 20? 20? Spring 2010.

Spring 20, 2009! Yes, that was it. Spring 20, 2009. That was the day. It was the day he had leapt through his run and found himself in Homehill. That was the day he met Higher and Digger; that was the day he came home. Yes, he'd been here a year, but was that something to get so excited about?

'One more bite, then I'm done,' said Freddy. 'Well that's it. Happy Homaday, Bounder! It's your first Homaday and there's nothing like the first one. The others are good, but the first one's always the best, especially for in-comers.'

'A Homaday? What's a Homaday? And why is the first one the best? I really don't know what you are talking about!'

'A Homaday,' said Freddy, 'is the day of the year we celebrate someone's home coming. It's a celebration of the day each bunny came to the warren. So today, bonny Bounder, is your Homaday. And the first one is always very special. You see – if you manage to stay in a warren for a year, without wandering away or getting eaten by a fox, or wooed by some other rabbit in some other warren, then you generally stay forever. You, precious Bounder, are the only in-coming rabbit that's celebrated their first Homaday in our warren for a long time.

'I was an in-born rabbit so I can't really remember mine because I was only a baby bunkins at the time. I've seen all the pictures taken by Higher and Digger and it looked such fun.

'And when you are an in-comer it becomes even more special. That's when Big Buck turns up to celebrate too. Oh! I can't wait to meet him.

'I've heard so much about him. But then, it'll be you

that's the star of the show, not me.'

Higher and Digger appeared.

'We're home again. How are the preparations going, Bounder? Are you washed and brushed yet? Digger has your special suit and I'll be ready for a pep-talk with you as soon as you're dressed,' said Higher.

'I've just finished breakfast,' said Bounder, swallowing his last mouthful. 'I'll go and shower and brush.'

Bounder reappeared. 'I'm ready now!' he said. He and Digger went back through to his bedroom. Digger produced a bag containing a smart outfit.

'Well, here you are; there's your suit and here's your shirt and tie. Do you still have that special tie-pin I gave you? Today's the day to polish it and display it proudly, so all can see and admire it.'

Bounder looked astonished. Display it proudly? Let people admire it? What was there to admire? Well, yes, the tie-pin itself was beautiful, admirable in fact, but Bounder had always been reluctant to wear it. It reminded him of the day when he'd eaten some of the awful mushroom. He wanted to forget that mistake, not boast about it.

'Can you find it? You've not had it on recently. You have to have it somewhere. You haven't lost it, have you, Bounder?'

'No, Digger. It's here in my drawer, but I don't really want to wear. . . .'

'Don't want to wear it? Of course you want to wear it.'

'But it reminds me that I wasn't a very clever rabbit and I shouldn't have. . . .'

'You made a little mistake; you ate a little bit of something that you shouldn't because you were hungry. What's wrong with that? We all get hungry. The main thing is you dived into Polka Dot Stream and found the cure.'

'I didn't dive in, I was. . . .'

'You went for the cure, you received the cure. That's all that matters, and I trust you'll not be eating polka dot mushrooms again.'

'Oh no, Digger. That's for sure. I'll go for the Polka Dot Stream and the grass round about it, any day.'

'Well, there you are then. You can wear this with pride,' said Digger, as he pinned the tie-pin to Bounder. He helped him into the pale tan jacket and put a big top hat on his head.

'All set. Now Higher can do her bit. He's all yours, my dear,' he called as they came out of the bedroom. Digger placed the forepaw of Bounder into the forepaw of Higher. She led Bounder out of the warren and up the hill.

'Well, Bounder. Happy Homaday, Homehill rabbit. Today marks your first year at our warren. We are so pleased you came to join us and we are looking forward to having you stay with us forever. Big Buck will be meeting with you at 11 o'clock and the feast begins at midday. How are you feeling, dear?' said Higher. 'Are you glad you stayed?'

'Did I have a choice?' said Bounder. 'When I tried to go back to Hutchanrun, it was not there. I remember that day well.'

'Yes,' said Higher. 'Remember it well. Were you glad? Were you sad? How did you feel that day, Bounder?'

Bounder replayed the story in his mind. He remembered the feelings he had when he saw the hutch had disappeared. Then he realised something. Yes, at the time he had thought it would be good to go back to Hutchanrun. The thought of ready-made food and water and a nice safe bed all made sense and it sounded like a good way to live BUT . . . (it was a big BUT) it was boring! There was no fun. It was all routine. One day after the other, all the same. The only change that happened was when he got cabbage leaves or lettuce instead of carrots. And he had longed so much for freedom. He had longed to be out in the open spaces.

He had always known there was something more. And now he had found it.

The freedom and excitement he had been looking for. Yes he'd had some scrapes and probably would have some more, but the good side was definitely better than the downside. He was where his heart belonged.

He looked at Higher. She was staring at him. He knew she was waiting for the answer.

'You need to say it dear,' she said. 'Not for my sake, but for yours. Were you glad? Were you sad? How did you feel?'

'Well,' said Bounder, 'when I first saw the empty garden, I was lost. I felt as though I had been abandoned and let down. I did not know what to do. I just wanted a safe place to be. And the place I thought was safe was not there anymore. Then you and Digger appeared. Oops! I was a bit mean to you that day wasn't I?'

Bounder went over to Higher and put his paws around her neck.

'I did not intend to be. I'm sorry. I was feeling sorry for myself and blamed it all on you. But then, when I saw you bounding up the hill, I realised that I wanted to go with you; that I belonged with you; that my home was not in Hutchanrun but in Homehill! You were way up the hill when I followed you but I caught you up. Hey, did you wait for me? Did you know I would follow? Would you really have left me?'

But as he took his paws away from around Higher's neck and looked into her eyes, he knew there was no way she was ever going to answer those questions.

'What if I'd stayed behind?'

'Well,' said Higher, 'Your carers in Hutchanrun know that once a bunny has a taste of freedom they can never be trusted to stay in their hutch again. That's why they took the hutch away. Only you know the answers to the other questions . . . but come, let's go and meet Big Buck. '

They walked along the path in silence. Bounder was deep in thought and Higher

was just enjoying his company. She
had come to think of Bounder as one of
her own and she had enjoyed watching
him change from a caged rabbit
into a wild one.

They came to a big oak
tree and Digger was there
waiting for them.

'OK, my love?' he said to
Higher. 'All done?'

'Yes,' said Higher 'all done.
Shall we go?'

Before she had finished
speaking, Bounder found he had one paw
in Digger's and one in Higher's. He was
being half carried, half swung up the hill

towards a place he'd never been before.

The grass was greener here and the smell so sweet it almost took your breath away. They came to a big rock and stopped. They set Bounder down and shouted,

'We're here, Big Buck.'

A loud, deep voice came from the other side of the rock. It was so loud that it made Bounder jump. It was so deep that he took a while to attune his ears to what it said.

'Come on round, my beloved ones. I'm waiting for you.' Bounder's knees began to tremble. Waiting? What for? He wondered. He was not sure if he wanted to meet the rabbit that belonged to the voice. It sounded quite awesome. But he did not get a chance to run away.

Higher and Digger led him round to the other side of the rock to meet Big Buck.

Bounder stood and stared. Then he fell on his face. Big Buck was awesome. He was big. He was a buck. He was rabbit. He was freedom. He was fun. He was serious. He was love. He was. . . .

Bounder found the best way to describe
Big Buck was that he was Rabbit; Rabbit with
a capital 'R'. He was everything Higher was,
but more so. He was everything
Digger was, but more so.
He was everything that
Bounder wanted himself
to be, but more so.
His name fitted him
perfectly; he was Big
Buck.
Bounder then felt
himself being lifted
up. Big Buck had
gently lifted him onto his
lap and was now cradling him

on his knee and singing to him. Bounder heard again those songs his mother had sung to him as a baby. He relaxed in Big Buck's arms and let the melodies go deep into his heart. He was a Homehill Bunny. He had come home.

Big Buck then lifted him gently down and set him on his paws.

'Well, young bunkin,' he said. 'I have some serious questions to ask. Please think very hard before you answer them, and make sure you give the correct answer. If you give the wrong answer there will be some very serious consequences.'

Bounder began to tremble. He looked down at his back paws. This was a very silly thing to do because if he had stayed looking into Big Buck's eyes he would have seen something that would have made him feel very differently.

Big Buck was looking at Bounder with such love and there was a twinkle in his eyes as he was talking. Bounder would have realised that the questions were not going to be that difficult. As it was, Bounder had visions of ending up as rabbit pie.

'Well, shall we begin?'

'OK,' squeaked Bounder.

'Question number one. Do you like it here in Homehill?' the big loud voice boomed.

'Yes,' said Bounder in a small whisper.

'Pardon?' said Big Buck, in a quieter, gentler voice. 'Did you say you liked it here?'

'Yes, I like it here,' said Bounder, this time a bit louder.

'Well done. That was a good answer. We can proceed. Question number two. Would you like to settle here, spend the rest of your days here?'

Bounder paused. He had not thought about the rest of his life. He had just been living day to day. He began to dream. It would be good to stay at Homehill, in the warren with Higher and Digger. It was safe and secure and they were always around to help him out of the scrapes he got himself into.

'Yes, that would be good,' he replied.

'Then you will need to dig your own warren. There's a space for you at the top of the road by Spreading-Oak tree. . .' Big Buck paused. He looked at Bounder.

Bounder was gaping at Big Buck with an open mouth. He looked as though the bottom had just fallen out of his world. If Big Buck had been able to read Bounder's mind, and perhaps he could, he would have seen that the young rabbit was trying to decide if it was possible to change his mind.

Would it be a good idea to take back his last reply? If he had to leave the security of Higher and Digger's warren did he still want to stay? If he had to move away from them, did he want to remain on Homehill? He was not sure.

'And you will need to continue to explore Homehill.

There are lots of places you haven't been to yet, lots of adventures for you to have and . . . but before I go on to that, you definitely said yes, didn't you? You don't want to leave, do you?'

Bounder had not been sure he wanted to stay if it meant leaving Higher and Digger's warren. When he realised the only other option was to leave Homehill, he knew he wanted to stay. Forever. He had enjoyed living with Higher and Digger. He had also enjoyed exploring. He had enjoyed meeting the other rabbits whose home was Homehill and yes, he wanted to stay. This hill had become home for him; there was nowhere else he wanted to go.

He looked up to Big Buck again. His eyes met Big Buck's eyes. This time he saw the love that had always been there and the twinkle in his eyes. Somehow Bounder knew he needed to voice those feelings that were springing up from deep within.

'Big Buck,' he said, this time in a loud, sure voice, 'there's nowhere else I want to live. There's nowhere else I want to go. This is where I've found my home; this is where I'll stay, forever. Adventures, here I come.' Bounder smiled and jumped as he spoke the last words.

Big Buck smiled too. Within Big Buck's smile was a look which seemed to say, you may not be so eager for adventures if you knew what they were going to be.

Big Buck was the only one with that knowledge and he certainly was not going to let Bounder into the secret. The fact that Bounder had expressed his desire to stay in Homehill was all he needed him to do at that time.

'Well then, let's go to the party, young fellow.'

Bounder found himself flying through the air. He landed on Big Buck's shoulders and was carried along as Big Buck leapt and bounded up the side of the hill.

From the top of the hill they could see to the other side, where there was a great celebration going on. Big Buck ran down the hill towards it.

There was a long table which had been laid out with all sorts of delicacies - green grass jelly, carrot ale, lettuce soup and a splendid cake with lots of sugary icing on top. As Bounder looked at the cake he saw the icing had a pattern to it.

He thought he could make out the shape of two rabbits holding hands. But when he looked again it just looked like a random pile of sugar. At the back of the table was a big banner saying, 'Happy Homaday Bounder, Welcome Home.'

Big Buck then lifted him down off his shoulders. Almost before his paws had touched the ground, Freddy bounded up to him.

'Happy Homaday, Bounder. Isn't it wonderful? You're going to stay and how do you like . . . umph'. Higher's paw had landed in his mouth.

'Come and sit down, Freddy,' she said, leading him away and whispering in his ear. Then Digger appeared and took Bounder by the paw.

'Come to your seat, Bounder,' he said as he led Bounder to the head of the table.

Higher and Digger sat on his left, with Freddy and the rest of their offspring next to them. Big Buck and his wife and family sat at his other side. Once everyone was seated Big Buck stood up.

He said, 'One! Two! Three!' and then it began. They all started to sing. What a sound filled the air, each rabbit singing at a pitch and with a harmony that suited them. The young rabbits were sopranos, the old bucks were bass and all the other rabbits were somewhere in between.

This is what they sang (to the tune of Happy Birthday):

'Happy Homaday to you;
Happy Homaday to you;
Happy Homaday, dear Bounder;
Happy Homaday to you.'

They gave him three cheers and then Big Buck shouted, 'Tuck in, folks,' and the feasting began. They chatted and ate and had a really good time.

Freddy kept leaning over to Bounder to begin to say something; but each time he got a dig in the ribs from Higher and a word in his ear from Digger. Bounder was aware that something was going on but was enjoying the food too much to wonder what it might be.

Once all the food had been eaten and the table was being cleared, he heard Higher whisper to Freddy,

'It's just about time, dear. The moment you've been waiting for.'

Bounder saw Freddy clap his paws in delight. Big Buck stood up. He took Bounder by the paw and led him round the table. Then they turned to face the guests.

'Let me introduce you to Bounder,' he said. 'It's his special day. He has decided to join us here in Homehill, and to make this his home, forever.'

A big cheer went up and a cry of welcome.

'As is the custom, we will have the three blessings and then I will give him the Homaday present.'

Blessings and a present! Bounder could hardly believe his ears. He'd never been given a present but he knew it was good. He did not know what blessings were but they also sounded good. And he was going to get three of them! He was delighted. So this is why Freddy was so excited.

Big Buck continued speaking. 'For the First Blessing, I call on Higher.'

Higher came round the table and put her paw on Bounder's shoulder.

'Isn't he a great bunny?' she addressed the crowd. 'I am so pleased to have met Bounder and have had him in my warren.' Then, turning to face Bounder, she said, 'We shall miss you when you move, dear Bounder. But remember, you will always be welcome to pay us a visit. We will always be around if you need us. Just shout, call, or whisper and we'll be there.'

Then she put a paw on each of his shoulders. The whole place became quiet and Bounder realised what was about to happen was very special.

'Bounder,' she said, looking into his eyes, 'I bless you. I bless you to be a Homehill rabbit, for the rest of your days. I bless you to know love, to receive it and to give it away. I bless you with the knowledge that you are a Homehill Bunny deep in your heart. I bless you to be a Homehill Bunny and to grow and expand in Homehill ways, to bring to life those songs your mother sang to you as a bunkin and to fulfil all that you were born to be.'

She stepped back and then Digger came over. He took up a similar stance to Higher and this was his blessing:

'Bounder, I bless you to be Bounder. I bless you to bound over the hills; may your paws be sure-paws and may you bound higher and farther than any Homehill rabbit has done before. I bless you to have a warren navigation system, so you will always know how to return home. I bless you with an ability to keep going, even when the path is hard and steep or deep and boggy.

'I bless you to be an explorer and a bunny that pushes back the boundaries. I bless you to fulfil your destiny, Bounder, my bunkins.'

As Digger stepped back, up came Freddy. 'I've only one word to say,' he whispered in Bounder's ears. Then he shouted, 'FREEDOM!' so loud that Bounder fell back on the floor and the hill shook with the sound. It seemed to echo round and round the hill and round and round his head. 'Freedom! Freedom! Freedom!'

He felt his heart would burst. This is what he'd longed for all his life. This is what he had dreamed about when he was a little bunny in Hutchanrun. Now his dreams had been fulfilled. He felt as though he was in heaven. He was content to stay there forever.

But the celebrations were not yet complete. There was a sound of music in the air and Big Buck came over to Bounder and pulled him to his feet.

'Just one more surprise, my bunkin,' he said. He held Bounder by the paw and they both faced the rest of the rabbits as Big Buck began his speech.

'Well, bucks, does and bunkins. What a day this has been. How great it is to have Bounder joining us. He has given his promise to stay with us, here in Homehill, so it gives me great pleasure to proceed to the next stage in the party.'

Bounder looked quizzically at Big Buck. Something else was going on. All the other rabbits gave a great cheer. They knew something he did not.

'Bounder, you have promised to join us here in Homehill, so it is my pleasure to give you the piece of ground under Spreading Oak for your warren. We shall expect you to live as befits a Homehill Rabbit and to grow in Homehillness and in family. To that end, it gives me great pleasure to give to you my youngest doe, Steffie, for your wife. May you have many happy years together and be blessed with lots and lots of bunkins.'

He then raised his voice and shouted,

'Steffie, come forth.'

She came forth. The most beautiful, delightful doe Bounder had ever seen. She glided majestically over to him; they held paws and then gave each other the biggest bunny hug you have ever seen. They kissed each other and fell head over paws in love.

The music began again, more carrot ale and lettuce wine was served and the celebrations continued. After an hour or so of dancing, the cake reappeared. Bounder and Steffie were given a knife and told to 'cut the cake 'cos we're craving for a crumb!' As Bounder looked at the cake he saw the two rabbits holding hands again. The buck had a B on his jacket and the doe had an S on her dress.

'Look, it's us,' said Steffie. 'It seems a shame to cut it. But we believe that as each bunny here eats a piece of the couple-cake, it is as though they are making us part of their family. They are making a promise to help us in our life together. Good, isn't it?'

Bounder and Steffie handed a piece of cake to each rabbit. In everyone's eyes there was a look of love and acceptance and pride. Bounder knew he had found his home, the love of his life and the place where he could settle and bring up his family. His future looked rosy. What a day it had been. Bounder may not have known what Freddy was talking about at the beginning of the day, but he had to admit, it was worth being woken up at six o'clock for.

Happy Homaday, Bounder, and may you have plenty more of them.

Chapter 6 | The Pool

Bounder and Steffie were enjoying the celebrations of Bounder's first Homaday when Big Buck came over to their table.

'Well,' he said, 'decide who's coming first and let's go.'

Steffie looked at Bounder and Bounder looked at Steffie. Neither knew where they were meant to be going and neither wanted to ask. Big Buck stood there. He looked from one to the other waiting for a reply. Bounder and Steffie spoke together:

'Ladies before Gentlemen!'

'Bucks lead the way!'

Big Buck laughed. 'Well, I didn't think I was that scary,' he said. 'Honest, I don't bite. But there is something you both have to do before you can begin your life together. It needs to be done by each of you in turn. I'll explain what it is when we're on the way. So who's coming first?'

They both started to get up, then all three began to laugh. Big Buck saw he would have to make the choice.

'Steffie, my lady,' said Big Buck, 'may I have the pleasure of your company?'

'Of course,' she replied and put her paw into his. She gave Bounder a quick kiss on his cheek and went away with Big Buck.

'See you later.'

'Once she's done I'll send her home' said Big Buck. 'Then I'll come back for you. See you shortly.'

Bounder watched the two of them as they disappeared up the hill, laughing and chatting as they went.

Bounder decided to look for Freddy. Perhaps he would know what was going on. He soon found him. Freddy was sitting with Higher and Digger and the rest of his family. Higher saw Bounder approaching and drew over another seat.

'Come and join us, dear,' she said. 'Don't worry; it'll soon be your turn.'

Then she carried on with her story. Bounder looked towards Freddy and mouthed, 'Where?' but Freddy only shrugged his shoulders. He knew a lot of things but not this.

Only grown-up rabbits knew about what was happening. Freddy leaned over to ask his father, but Digger only put his paw to his mouth to indicate he was not allowed to say.

Poor Bounder. He was having a very happy day. He had had lots of surprises and he enjoyed them all. But he was still not quite at ease in Big Buck's company. He just seemed too Rabbit, too much of what Bounder knew he wanted to be, but wasn't. Higher carried on with her story so Bounder's thoughts soon turned from himself and Big Buck into the story she was telling.

Big Buck returned and touched him on the shoulder. Bounder jumped. Big Buck whispered into his ear

'Now, my dear chap, it's your turn; are you ready?'

Bounder got off his seat, waved a quick goodbye to Freddy and set off with Big Buck. They began to climb up the hill towards the back of the party and then went on a path through a wood. Bounder had never been this way before but he didn't get much chance to admire the view or to work out exactly where he was going.

Big Buck engaged him in conversation. 'Well, Bounder,' he said. 'It is so good to have you here at Homehill. I can remember when your grandma was in our warren. What a beautiful doe she was! She really enjoyed living here and I was so pleased when I knew you were down in Hutchanrun.

'Did you know I came to your house every night? I couldn't wait for the day when you were free. Oh it was so exciting; I had Digger and

Higher ready to find you when you first came here. I was so pleased that you enjoyed their company and said that you would join them. I just hopped and skipped and danced all night. I was so excited.

'And I have been counting the days till your first Homaday. When Steffie was born I knew she was just the doe for you. I couldn't wait for her to grow up and for you to be free. You will make a lovely couple, you know.'

Big Buck stopped and turned and looked at Bounder. Bounder stopped walking too and stood, mouth open, looking at Big Buck.

'What is it, my bunkins?' said Big Buck.

Bounder replied, 'You said you knew me in Hutchanrun, but I never met you till today, did I? I'm sure I've not seen you before.'

Big Buck smiled. 'Well, maybe not seen,' he said, 'but you do know me. Remember the songs? Remember the longings in your heart?'

'You had something to do with those?' asked Bounder.

'Everything,' said Big Buck as he lifted Bounder's chin and looked into his eyes. 'Absolutely everything.'

Something in Bounder's heart softened towards Big Buck as he pondered on what had just been said. If Big Buck was part of those longings, if Big Buck was somehow in those songs his mother used to sing, then Big Buck couldn't be all that scary.

Bounder continued to think about what Big Buck had said as they climbed up the hill. He remembered the longings in his heart when Hutchanrun had been his home. He thought back over some of his adventures in Homehill and

he remembered the day he had wished he could go back and stay in Hutchanrun.

'Well,' said Big Buck, 'You have had a few adventures, haven't you? And there's more to come. Remember there's always help at hand. You just need to call and it will arrive. You'll never be alone in Homehill. We are all here beside you. You've always been a Homehill rabbit and always will be; Hutchanrun was never your true home. Bounder's your name and you'll always be one for adventure. Be ready for all that comes your way.

Do you think you'll like Steffie?'

'Steffie,' said Bounder. 'Steffie, she's beautiful, she's wonderful. I love her with all my heart. I'm looking forward to building up a warren with her. Thank you, Big Buck, for giving her to me.'

'My pleasure,' said Big Buck. 'And this is why I've brought you here. Before you set up home you need to take a dip in Purifying Pool. I'll tell you the story and then you'll understand the reason:

'It happened a long time ago. A stranger called Ritchie Rabbit came to Homehill and joined the warren. He was smart, beautiful and strong and many of the does fell in love with him. He fathered many bunkins and we enjoyed having him around. However, after a few springs passed things began to go very wrong.

'We found that all his bunkins lost their love for Homehill. They decided they did not like the running streams. They wanted to build dams and turn them into still pools. They complained the grass was coarse and hard to chew and they began to fight each other.

'Then it became even worse. Their fur lost its shine, their noses ran, they became very ill and began to die. Instead of fun and freedom, fear and death surrounded the warren. I did not know what had happened or what to do about it. Many of the rabbits went to live in Hutchanrun, others just died. Our warren got smaller and smaller.

'I spent many evenings talking with My Doe about how we could save the warren. We realised things started to change when Ritchie had come. So we asked him to go. I was surprised that he left without a fight and we thought our problems were over. They were not. Things did not get any better.

'Later I learnt that he had infected us with a deadly disease and there was nothing we could do to stop it spreading throughout the whole warren. I began to search for a cure. I went throughout the whole of Homehill but no one I spoke to knew the answer until. . . .

'Well here we are; here it is; beautiful isn't it?'

They had stopped at the side of a big, deep pool of murky-looking water. Bounder stared, first at the pool, then at Big Buck. The pool was set in a hollow and at the far side of it was a little shelter. Bounder thought it looked a bit like one of the wishing wells he had seen in a neighbour's garden in Hutchanrun. But it wasn't as pretty. It was a plain brown colour and certainly not what Bounder could describe as beautiful. They walked round the pool to the shelter.

It was indeed like a wishing well and Big Buck was turning the handle. Before too long a basket appeared, full of the reddish-brown dirty-looking water. Big Buck lifted it onto the ground beside the pool and turned to Bounder.

'Well, in you get and I'll lower you down into the depths. Remember to keep hold of the sides and keep your eyes open. Just breathe normally and you'll be fine. It takes about two minutes. Then you'll be ready to go and set up warren.'

'You expect me to get into that?' asked Bounder, looking at Big Buck in amazement. 'I can't do that, it's awful, it's dirty and smelly and what about my nice new suit?'

'Oh, sorry. I forgot to say, you need to get undressed first, of course you do. I'll keep guard over your clothes, don't worry about that.'

Bounder looked again. First at the pool, then at the basket and then at Big Buck. Big Buck did not look as though he was joking; in fact he looked very serious. The basket was certainly big enough for Bounder to climb into, so he could not say he would not fit. Very slowly he began to undress himself. Big Buck continued with his story.

'I didn't finish, did I? I had a dream one night. I dreamt that I went to the northern edge of Homehill and fell into this pool. I felt as though I was going to drown. As I began to sink lower and lower, I realised I could still breathe. I opened my eyes and I could see.

'Do you know what I saw? I saw each of my rabbits in Homehill. They were laughing and hopping and jumping. They were dancing like we used to dance

and partying like we used to party. Not one of them was ill. In fact they looked healthier and more alive than I'd ever seen them. It was great. I was so happy. I began to laugh and laugh. As I laughed I began to rise again and I came back up to the top of the water and climbed out. I believed in that dream I found the cure.

'So the following day, I packed up a bag and set out to find the pool. I knew that if it was real then I had found the answer to our problems; the cure for our disease. I wandered over the hills to the edge of Homehill. Here it was, just as I had seen it. I jumped in and sank into the depths. It felt so refreshing and so cleansing. I felt so alive. I took a big leap out and ran all the way back home. I gathered all the rabbits from Homehill together and told them about my dream and the pool.

'We called the next day a holiday and invited everyone to come and bathe in the pool. It was great fun. We had a party! Young and old diving down into the pool. Then coming up with life in their eyes and hope in their hearts. My heart was fit to burst.

'That was it. Homehill came back to life again: the illnesses stopped, the complaining stopped, the fighting stopped. The dams that had been built to stop the flow of the streams were destroyed and it was as though Ritchie Rabbit had never been with us. I thought that everything was OK.

'What I hadn't realised was that some rabbits ignored my invitation. A few generations later we had more fighting, more illnesses, more of Ritchie's ways. The rabbits that had not been in the pool had passed their illness down to their bunkins and greatbunkins.

'This meant that I had to keep the invitations going. I made a rule that rabbits who wanted to stay in Homehill had to come and bathe in the Pool. Those who were not willing to do so were asked to leave.

'So now I make sure that any rabbit that is going to start a new warren comes here for a bath. That includes you, so off you go, Bounder. Into the basket!'

Bounder had enjoyed listening to Big Buck's story. His heart had jumped for joy at the thought of being free and healthy for the rest of his life and of having healthy bunkins.

He still did not like the idea of getting into the basket and going down into the murky waters. Big Buck sensed this and offered Bounder a paw to help him into the basket.

'Steffie's been down into the Pool,' he said, 'and she is at Spreading Oak. It's not a good idea to keep your doe waiting too long!'

Bounder thought of Steffie. He longed to be with her again and realised that would only be possible after this bath. He thought of her beauty as he climbed into the basket and held on tight as Big Buck lowered him into the pool.

Two minutes later he was back at the surface again.

'Wow!' he said, as Big Buck helped him climb out again. 'That water's amazing! Polka Dot Stream times ten!' He shook himself dry and put on his suit again.

'Great, isn't it?' said Big Buck.

'Unforgettable!' said Bounder.

'Well, Bounder, if Steffie's to know you are unforgettable too, you'd better hurry away now. Happy Homaday, Bounder, and happy life together!'

'Thanks, Big Buck,' said Bounder as he bounded down the hill to join his doe and start out on their life together.

To be continued. . . .

MUSIC FOR SONGS

My Place Of Rest

Arr. by Heather Turner

Penny Shackleton

Version 2

126

Arr. Heather Turner

Exploring Homehill

Penny Shackleton

I'm a Home-hill bun-ny on the run, I'm ex - plor-ing the hills,

oh what fun, with a run, with a jump, With a leap and with a bound, I'm a - mazed at the things I have

found. Wat - er that's a - live flow-ing down and down, Sweet-est tast-ing grass

grow-ing all a-round, Flow-ers fair, , trees so tall, Help ar - riv-ing when you call, Life has joy, it's a thrill, In this

place that's called Home-hill. Where our hearts find their rest and are still.

A WORD FROM THE AUTHOR

Hi,

I live in the kingdom of Fife and work as a health care professional in the local hospitals. I have been involved in children's work in various churches since I was a teenager and love reading and telling stories. More recently I began to write my own stories and created Bounder and his friends in Homehill. Like him, I love exploring in the countryside and climbing hills. And like him I have found the freedom to be myself and enjoy this adventure that we call life, will all its ups and downs. These stories reflect some of my own experiences.

The characters in this book have their own website: **www.homehillfriends.co.uk**
It contains the accompaniment for the songs and other Homehill resources and fun pages. I hope you will visit it to find out more and continue the adventure.

Penny